Rascal

SWEPT BENEATH THE WATERS

D1102076

Collect all of Rascal's adventures:

 RASCAL: LOST IN THE CAVES

 RASCAL: TRAPPED ON THE TRACKS

 RASCAL: RUNNING FOR HIS LIFE

 RASCAL: FACING THE FLAMES

 RASCAL: SWEPT BENEATH THE WATERS

 RASCAL: RACING AGAINST TIME

Rascal

SWEPT BENEATH THE WATERS

CHRIS COOPER

ILLUSTRATED BY JAMES DE LA RUE

EGMONT

EGMONT

We bring stories to life

First published as *Tramp: Swept Beneath the Waters* by Puffin in 2004
This edition first published in Great Britain in 2015
by Egmont UK Limited
The Yellow Building, 1 Nicholas Road, London W11 4AN

Text copyright © 2004 Chris Cooper ·
Illustration copyright © 2015 James de la Rue
The moral rights of the author and illustrator have been asserted

ISBN: 978 1 4052 7532 3

58628/1

www.egmont.co.uk

A CIP catalogue record for this title is available from the British Library

Typeset by Avon DataSet Ltd, Bidford on Avon, Warwickshire
Printed and bound in Great Britain by CPI Group

MIX
Paper
FSC FSC® C018306

For Cathy, Sam
and Sophie

CHAPTER 1

Rascal came to the river in the grey light of early morning.

He'd been on the move since before sunrise and he had made good time. But what now? To continue his journey west, he had to cross to the other side.

The river wasn't too wide, but its level was high after several days of rain and its waters ran fast. A feeling of uneasiness clutched at the dog. Could he swim in such a strong current?

Rascal didn't want to find out. A shiver of fear ran through him at the very thought. He looked up and down the river. One direction led off to nothing but wilderness. In the other, he could make out electricity pylons in the distance. That meant a town. Usually Rascal tried to avoid towns as much as possible — it was safer that way — but he knew there was a better chance of finding a bridge in that direction. He began to follow the river downstream.

The trees around him had started to lose their leaves. A memory stirred in Rascal's mind of playing with Joel in the back garden. He had been no more than a puppy then. Joel had promised his parents that he would rake up the leaves that littered the lawn. And he had made good on that promise, until . . .

'Check this out, Rascal!' Joel had said with a grin. And then he had scooped up a handful of the leaves and tossed them into the air.

'Its raining leaves!' Joel had laughed,

and Rascal had been happy to join
in the fun, jumping up and barking
excitedly.

'What are you two up to out there?'
had come the cry from the kitchen
window. But, as boy and dog rolled in
the leaf pile, Joel had been laughing too
hard even to answer his mum.

But Joel was far away now and the

falling leaves filled the dog with anxiety.
Autumn was here. He could feel it on
the wind, like a promise of the winter to
come. What if he hadn't made it home
before the really bad weather set in? He
would never be able to continue his
journey once the first snows had fallen.

And then what?

The river curved round, and beyond
the bend a small road ran alongside it.
Rascal was able to pick up speed now,
running in the middle of the road but
always keeping the river in sight. He
didn't even notice the sound of an
engine behind him until the blare of

a horn startled him. It was loud and it
didn't sound like car horns usually did.
This one played a few notes of music.

Rascal leapt to the side of the road
just in time before a battered red pickup
truck roared by. The man in the driver's
seat shouted something through the
open window. Rascal watched until the

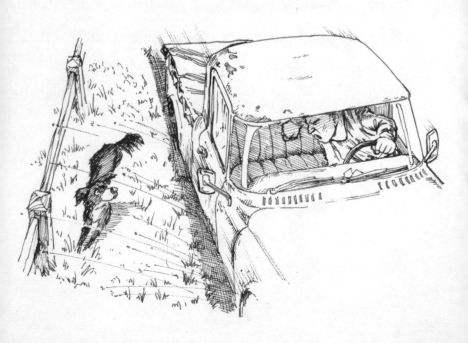

truck disappeared round the bend ahead.

He continued more carefully now. Soon he passed a few warehouses by the water's edge. And then the land opened up in front of him. He had come to a small park that sloped up from the river. At the far end of the park lay a small town . . . and also a footbridge across the river.

He would be able to cross here.

As he set off in the direction of the bridge, Rascal became aware of the one vehicle parked at the top of the hill alongside the park. It was the red pickup truck, the same one that had passed him on the road earlier. But where was the driver now?

The answer came moments later when a burly man burst out from behind the park's wooden shelter, down near the waterfront. He was in his mid-twenties, with hair cropped close to his head. His face was set in a grimace, as if he wanted to get out of this place as fast as possible.

Over the past few months, Rascal had learned to read humans. It was a matter of survival. With some you could sense their kindness – it almost shone from them like a light. But there were other people Rascal now knew he had to avoid. It had been a hard lesson to learn. Such people cared nothing about a stray dog like him. If he tried to beg a bite to eat from one of them, he was more likely to receive a snarled insult or even a kick for his troubles.

Rascal was sure of one thing: this man belonged to the second kind. And for the man to get back to his truck at the top of the hill, he would have to go right by Rascal. Fear stabbed at the dog.

Rascal did his best to disappear into himself, to not look up, to act as if he wasn't there at all.

'I can't get away from stinkin' dogs,'

snarled the man, when he neared the path Rascal was on. The stale smell of cigarettes was strong on him and . . . something else too, but Rascal couldn't place the scent.

'Beat it!' yelled the man.

Rascal scurried quickly out of range of the boot that lashed his way.

The man ran right past him and up the hill. He pulled open the truck door and soon the engine roared into life. The man revved it a few times and then, with a squeal of wheels on concrete, the truck disappeared down the road.

The dog padded forwards carefully.

The man was gone, but Rascal's senses told him that he was not alone in this park. He sniffed the air, finally identifying the scent. He knew it! There was another dog close by, maybe more than one.

But where?

It was only chance that the wind died down at the right moment for Rascal to hear the whimper. It sounded small and frightened, and it came from a line of bushes at the back of the shelter the man had emerged from.

Rascal edged closer. He heard the whimper again, this time joined by another. He pushed his snout through the bushes and saw a canvas bag lying on the other side. An acrid trace of cigarette smell hung around the bag and Rascal knew instantly that the man in the red pickup truck must have left this here.

The top of the bag was open and a tiny snout was poking out.

It was a puppy, a little black-and-brown dog so young that its fur was still fluffy.

Carefully, Rascal nudged the puppy back and then pulled on the opening of the bag. There were two other puppies in there, these ones even tinier than the

first. They were snuggling next to each other for warmth.

Rascal looked around but could see no other dog anywhere . . . no mother.

These puppies were all alone.

CHAPTER 2

Rascal gave them a reassuring lick, but that wasn't what these puppies wanted. Their whimpers became more urgent. The sound could mean only one thing: they were hungry. They needed food right away.

That was a feeling Rascal knew only too well. He looked up at the town that lay just beyond the park. If he went there to try to find some food for these puppies, he might be seen and caught. And if that happened, he might never get to see Joel again.

And yet . . . He looked down at the three little puppies. The biggest and most adventurous of them, the one that had been poking its nose out of the bag, was rubbing its head against Rascal's front leg.

How could he leave them like this? They seemed completely helpless. It was impossible to say how long they would survive without food.

There was nothing for it. Rascal nudged the bigger puppy back inside and did his best to close the bag up. Then he ran towards the town ahead, his extra burst of speed making him realise how tired and hungry he was himself.

Rascal didn't cross the bridge. Instead, he explored the alley behind a row of shops on this side of the river. Between two of them sat a large grey bin. It was stuffed full of rubbish and there were several other black plastic bags on the ground next to it.

He sniffed at the bags and his nose was attacked by a jumble of different food smells. Most of them weren't very appealing – at least not to Rascal's nose – but through all the bad smells he could tell there was meat somewhere. He sniffed again and identified which bag the good smell was coming from. He pawed at it. When this didn't help, he took hold of the plastic with his teeth and pulled. The bag ripped open and spilled its contents.

The good smell was coming from a big flat box that Rascal now pushed open with his snout. It contained several slices of old pizza with round bits of cooked meat on them.

The hunger in his own belly sprang to life. It had been a long time since Rascal had eaten . . . too long. He took a bite from one of the slices. The meat was too spicy and the base was stale, but his stomach was still grateful.

He was just finishing the last of the slice of pizza when the back door to one of the buildings opened. A man appeared, carrying another rubbish bag. He was wearing a white jacket that was spattered with food stains.

For an instant their eyes locked. Rascal tensed to run, but then the man smiled.

'You must be starving if you'll eat that,' he said. He knelt down and held out his

hand in a friendly gesture. 'Here, boy,' he said.

Usually Rascal would have loved to stick around. He could tell that this man was the sort who would find him something better to eat.

But the puppies were waiting for him back at the park. Rascal picked up the largest slice of pizza in his teeth, resisting the urge to bite down.

'It's OK. I won't hurt you,' said the man at the door, but Rascal was already running back.

He made it to the park as quickly as he could, taking care not to drop the food or let it trail along the ground. When he reached the bushes by the shelter, he set the slice of pizza down on the ground and pushed his way again to the canvas bag. He moved the top of the bag gently with his jaws . . . and looked down at the two puppies inside.

Two puppies!

The biggest of the three was no longer in the bag.

Rascal backed out of the bushes as fast as he could. The other puppy couldn't have gone far, could it?

He scanned the park quickly but saw nothing. He turned his attention back to the bushes. Perhaps it had crawled in deeper? But then he heard a small sound from behind him, a little yap of curiosity. It was coming from beside the river.

Anxiety pressed down on Rascal like a terrible weight. He started towards the river, unable to see the puppy beyond a line of plants at the edge of the park lawn. Suddenly there was another noise – this time a yelp of surprise and alarm.

Rascal felt a jolt of fear run through him like lightning. He raced to the river's edge.

At first he saw nothing in the murky water. But then a tiny head broke above the surface. It was the little puppy and it was terrified. It let out a panicked yelp and then disappeared back under again.

A torrent of fear swept through Rascal. Just the sight of the struggling puppy brought back terrible memories. It was in the black waters of an underground river that Rascal had been separated from his master, Joel. The dog had been lucky to survive. Even now, months later,

he could still remember the icy currents
that had battled to drag him below
the surface. He would never forget the
dreadful helpless feeling as that jet-black
water had poured into his mouth and
nose.

Rascal looked around in alarm. If only
there was someone he could alert, a
person who would know what to do, a
human who could help . . . Perhaps the
man he had seen in the alleyway? But a
line of trees blocked Rascal's view that
way, and there was no time to go back
to see if the man was still around.

He would have given anything not

to have to do this, but there was no alternative. The puppy was going to drown unless . . .

Rascal took a deep breath and jumped in.

CHAPTER 3

The next instant Rascal's world was once again one of coldness and dark. He tried to avoid becoming fully submerged in the water, but this was impossible and his head went under for a second or two. His feet did not touch the bottom – the

river was deeper than it looked – but he felt weeds of some kind brush against him.

Rascal could see the puppy's head bobbing up above the surface of the water ahead of him. He began to paddle frantically towards it, knowing that he would have to go faster than the current if he was to catch up.

His heart began to hammer. Already his own wet fur felt as if it was pulling him down. The puppy was close now, but then suddenly it disappeared beneath the waters. And this time it didn't come back up.

As both dogs approached the bridge,
Rascal did not even notice that two
people were standing there, watching
the drama in the river. One of them
was the man who had been in the alley
– he must have been curious enough
to follow the stray dog. The other was
a woman in a business suit. Wide-eyed

with fear, they followed events from the bridge.

It was too late for anyone else to help now. Rascal sucked in a deep gulp of air and plunged his head under the surface. Cold water stabbed at his eyes. It was almost impossible to see anything in the darkness, but he could just about make out something ahead of him, a deeper patch of black in the murky river.

Rascal pushed forwards and took hold of the small, black figure. Water poured into his mouth and his lungs, but he battled his way upwards and burst out into the air. He had the puppy by the back of its neck, but the little dog had fallen quiet. It hung limp and bedraggled in his mouth. Was Rascal too late?

He turned towards the bank. He had to keep his own head much higher out of the water now, so that the puppy did not slip below the surface again. This, combined with the difficulty of swimming against the current, made the going much tougher. With the puppy held between his jaws, it was harder and harder to breathe, but his body demanded oxygen. Rascal's lungs and muscles screamed. His legs began to feel as if they were weighted down.

At last he reached the bank. He gave
a final kick with his back legs and
managed to flop the puppy forwards on
to dry land. What he couldn't do was get
out of the water himself, as the bank was
just too high. It was an effort even to
stay in the same place here with his head
above water.

But then he heard a shout of concern.

'Here! I can see it! It's still in the
water.'

It was a man's voice, the man from the
alley. Moments later, strong arms were
lifting him to safety. The man set the dog
down carefully. Rascal didn't have the

energy even to shake the water from his
soaked fur.

Next to the man who had pulled
Rascal out, the woman was cradling the
puppy in her hands.

'I think it's going to be OK,' she
said urgently, 'but we'd better get it
somewhere warm, where it can be taken

care of properly.'

'This one too,' said the man, nodding at Rascal. 'I've never seen a dog do anything like that before.' He reached out and stroked Rascal's head.

Rascal's eyes closed and he swayed on his feet. The man's friendly touch was almost too much. There was nothing he wanted more than to let someone take care of him again, if only for a short while. To be given a proper meal, to be shown to a nice warm spot in front of a fire. He could almost feel the warmth on his back already . . .

Rascal's eyes snapped open with a

start. The other two puppies! If he let himself be taken away now, there was a chance that no one would find the other two puppies that were still in the park.

The woman was holding the puppy in the crook of one arm now as she spoke into her phone.

'Hello?' she said. 'Can you put me through to someone in animal welfare? Yes, this is an emergency.'

It took nearly all his remaining strength, but Rascal began to pull away from the man's hand.

'Where are you going now, boy?' said the man, watching as Rascal moved unsteadily back towards the park.

The man paused, unsure what to do, but finally he followed.

It wasn't a long way back to the park, but it seemed like miles to Rascal now. It was a battle to take each new step rather than just lie down to rest.

Finally he was there. Rascal staggered the remaining way to the bushes. The leftover food lay untouched where he had dropped it. He grabbed the bag in his teeth and tugged it part-way out of the bush. From inside, the plaintive cry of the puppies grew louder.

With a final glance over his shoulder

to see that the man was still following, Rascal let tiredness overtake him and he collapsed to the ground.

CHAPTER 4

Several hours later and many miles
away, Rascal's owner, Joel, stood with a
telephone in his hand. Before he dialled
the number, he told himself not to
get his hopes up. That was easier said
than done, of course. He felt a tingle of

excitement as the phone rang.

'Hello. Is that Mrs Armstrong?' he said when a woman answered. 'My name is Joel Holland. I'm calling about my dog.'

He launched into his explanation, telling her how he had lost Rascal all those months ago; how he had thought the dog was dead, until he had seen the news report about the forest fire. The reporter had spoken to a family called the Armstrongs, and there with them was Rascal. *His* Rascal.

Joel's mum had managed to track down a number for the television channel. At first they had refused to pass

on the Armstrongs' telephone number
to Joel, saying it was against their policy
to give out any personal numbers. But
after a couple of other long calls, they
had promised to contact the Armstrongs
themselves. If the family agreed, then
Joel could have their number.

Mrs Armstrong listened carefully now
to the whole story before saying in a
gentle voice, 'And . . . you're sure it was
the same dog?'

Of course, that question had echoed
around Joel's mind. But then he thought
about the alert look in those deep dark
eyes, the tufted ears that Rascal would

raise quizzically, the white pattern at the end of the black dog's muzzle.

It was the same dog, all right.

He simply said, 'Yes, I'm sure.'

Something in the boy's tone of voice convinced Mrs Armstrong.

'Well, after that day in the forest, you can imagine we were happy for him to stay with us,' she began. 'You must have heard what happened. If it hadn't been for Champion . . .' She caught herself. 'I'm sorry. I mean, if it hadn't been for Rascal . . . well, I don't like to think about what might have happened.'

Joel understood. The report on the

news had said that the Armstrong family had been trapped in a forest fire.

'Our vet couldn't find a microchip, so we assumed he had no owner,' continued Mrs Armstrong. 'I felt the very least we could do was give him a home. But he only stayed with us for a few days and all that time he seemed restless. Then one morning we got up and he was gone. He'd dug a hole under the fence in our front yard. We drove around the neighbourhood for hours and we checked all the animal shelters in the area, but there was no sign of him.'

Joel felt a brief stab of hopelessness.

He thanked Mrs Armstrong for her help. She took his number and promised to get in touch if she heard any further news about Rascal.

'And Joel?' she added.

'Yes?'

'He'll be OK,' she reassured him. 'He's a very special dog, you know.'

'I know . . . Thank you.'

After he'd put the phone down, Joel blinked back hot tears of frustration. More than anything, he felt angry with himself. He had known that it was too much to hope for, but part of him had been clinging to the idea that

Rascal would simply be there with the Armstrong family. He had even daydreamed about being able to hear the dog's friendly bark in the background.

Now he faced the cold truth. Rascal was no longer with the Armstrongs. He could be anywhere.

Joel looked again at the map of the country that he'd stuck to the wall

over his desk. He had marked with a coloured pin the spot where he and Rascal had been parted. Another pin marked the spot where Rascal had been with the Armstrong family.

The distance between the two pins represented a long, long way. Was it really possible for a lone dog to travel so far? It might happen in stories and films, but it couldn't in real life. Or could it? Joel reminded himself that it *was* possible. He had researched it at the school library. There *were* records of a few special dogs that had travelled across huge distances to be reunited with their owners.

Well, Mrs Armstrong was right –
Rascal was a special dog too. If he had
managed to get so far, surely he could
complete the remainder of his westward
journey.

CHAPTER 5

The rest of the day's events had passed in a blur to Rascal. Once all three puppies had been found, a uniformed worker from the animal shelter had arrived. She listened intently to the story of the puppy's rescue from the river.

Despite his weariness, Rascal's first thought was to try to make his escape – he didn't want to end up in the dog shelter – but a collar had been slipped around his neck. His chance of escape had gone.

He made no protest as he was led to the van and into a cage at the back of it. The blanket there felt like the most comfortable thing in the world at that moment. A few minutes later, the animal shelter officer carried the three puppies to the van. She placed the smaller two by Rascal, while she took out a blanket for the wet puppy. Sensing the warmth

of the bigger dog, the two crawled towards Rascal and tucked themselves in against his fur.

The shelter worker smiled broadly. 'Make yourselves at home, why don't you?'

Then, seeing that Rascal didn't mind sharing the cage space, she left them there and took the third puppy to the front seat. Her colleague started the van up.

'Back to the shelter?' he asked.

The woman shook her head. 'These puppies aren't old enough. They can't be more than a few weeks old,' she answered. 'They need round-the-clock care. I think they'd be better off with one of our foster parents.'

She spent the next few minutes speaking into a mobile phone, explaining the situation to the person on the other end of the line. When she put the phone down, there was relief in her voice.

'Good news,' she said. 'Judy will take them.'

Twenty minutes later, the van pulled

up outside a small house on a quiet street. A middle-aged woman was waiting at the door for them.

'They're tiny!' she exclaimed when she saw the puppies. Then she added with a hint of anger, 'Who'd go and abandon these?'

The woman called Judy looked at Rascal. 'What about the big dog?'

The man from the shelter shrugged. 'No collar or working microchip, so I suppose we'll just take him back to the shelter. Hope that someone's looking for him and gives us a call.' He didn't sound too optimistic about the chances of this happening.

Judy watched the puppies as they snuggled against Rascal's fur and the bigger dog gave one an affectionate lick.

'Well . . . I guess I could keep him here – overnight at least,' she suggested. 'I mean, the puppies seem to like him . . .'

And so Rascal avoided being taken to the animal shelter. Instead, he too was led inside the woman's house, where she had set up the laundry room beyond the kitchen for the puppies. She put the three of them into a cardboard box which she had lined with newspaper. A heating pad hung down on one side of the box and the three puppies all moved towards it. She then spread a blanket on the bare floor next to the box for Rascal.

'I'll get you something to eat just as soon as I've helped the little ones,' she said to him.

It was clear why. All three puppies were restless now. Their cries had become more and more urgent, and Rascal knew they had to feed their empty bellies.

This turned out to take longer than expected. Judy had placed a shallow pan of gruel-like food on the floor in the puppies' box, but none of the three made any move towards it.

The woman reappeared minutes later with a plastic bottle in her hand. She picked up the biggest of the puppies, holding it under its tummy with one hand. With the other hand, she gently parted the puppy's mouth and slipped the end of the bottle in.

It took a while, but at last the puppy began to suck at the milk formula.

'That's better, isn't it?' cooed Judy softly.

No wonder they hadn't touched the food Rascal had brought them. These puppies still needed their mother's milk,

at least for part of their diet.

Judy fed the other two puppies. It took even longer with these, and for the last one more formula seemed to dribble down Judy's hand than go inside its mouth. Judy frowned.

At last, when all three had been fed and were fast asleep in a corner of their box, Judy brought Rascal a bowl of food.

'You get the best dog food in the house,' she said with a grin. 'It's the least I can do after you've been so patient!'

Once the smell reached his snout, Rascal could be patient no longer. He

began to gobble
down the food.

As he ate, he
could hear Judy
talking in the
kitchen. Every so
often she paused, which meant she was
on the telephone.

'They're sleeping now,' she was
saying. 'They're old enough to make
a start on solids. I don't think any of
them have been weaned yet. I managed
to get a little formula down all three
of them, but not as much as I'd have
liked. It's early days yet, they may

improve. Best thing by far would be if you could find the mother, of course, but I don't suppose there's much chance of that.'

The rest of the day revolved around the three puppies and their needs. Judy checked on them regularly, changing the newspaper at the bottom of the box when necessary. She fed them once more at the end of the afternoon. Again she frowned at how little she was able to get them to drink.

Although they were of an age when most puppies are ready to explore the world around them, these three spent most of their time curled up and sleeping. Because Judy didn't want to leave them alone for long, she didn't take Rascal for a walk. Instead she opened the door to the back garden and let him spend a while out there.

This was the routine for the rest of the day. When night fell, the puppies slept, but their sleep was restless. Every

time Rascal came close to nodding off himself, their whimpers woke him up again. Their helplessness tugged at his heart.

Finally, Rascal padded over to the box. There was only just enough room, but he settled in next to the puppies. Instinctively, all three pressed themselves against his body. Once they had made themselves comfortable on him, their sleep became deeper and deeper.

But Rascal could not sleep. It wasn't only the cramped box or the three little bodies leaning against him. A mix of new feelings ran through him.

Rascal was just a young dog – not
too much more than a pup himself in
some ways – but these tiny creatures
aroused a different sort of feeling inside
him, a desire to keep them safe from
harm.

As well as this, a feeling of anger
was growing inside of him. Before the
puppies were bathed, Rascal had been
able to detect the same bitter smell on
them as he had on that bag: cigarette
smoke. Rascal remembered it was the
same smell he had noticed on the man
in the park, the one who had been so
eager to run back to his truck.

There was no other explanation. The man must have taken the puppies from their mother and then abandoned them there. As far as he knew, they might all be dead by now. It was simple luck that Rascal had found them.

Another thought followed this one. These pups needed their mother – but to find her, Rascal would first have to find the man with the red truck. But how? Finally, Rascal's weariness got the better of his anger and he drifted off to sleep.

It felt as if he had slept for just a few seconds, but it must have been more because he woke to the pale light of dawn. Sounds of movement came from the kitchen next door. Judy must be up and getting the puppies' first feed of the day ready.

Rascal carefully nudged one of the puppies off his forelegs and stood. After a long stretch, he padded to the window and looked out at the back garden.

'Need to go outside, do you?' asked Judy, opening the kitchen door. She was carrying the bottles of formula.

Rascal bounded outside. He took a last look back, to where Judy was already holding one of the puppies and giving it the bottle.

He felt a twinge of regret that he was leaving the puppies behind, but he knew they were in good hands. And if he stayed, there wasn't much he could do to help.

He looked towards the fence. It was quite high and his legs still ached with stiffness after a poor night's sleep. But what else could he do? He began to run. It was a short distance but he sprinted hard. He was going fast when he jumped. He sailed over the fence without even brushing a paw against it. As soon as he landed on the pavement, he looked around quickly to

see if his escape had been noticed.
It hadn't.

Rascal glanced westward. He knew
that, if he wanted, he could just carry
on now, continue his long journey

home. But then he would be leaving the puppies without their mother, and he could not do that.

Rascal headed towards the town.

CHAPTER 6

He wandered around town for hours. Even though he had seen the short-haired man for only a few seconds in the park, his scent was imprinted on the dog's mind. But Rascal did not see the man once that day and nor did he spot the red pickup truck.

Rascal began in the park – there was no one there but a young mother pushing a baby in a pram – and then moved into the town, finally using the footbridge to cross to the western side. He avoided the busier roads, but he roamed in and out of side streets in his search.

It was hopeless. Tired and hungry, Rascal flopped to the ground. The clouds above were grey and heavy. They matched the dog's mood. How was he ever going to find the puppies' mother?

He rested his head wearily on his front

paws. He was almost ready to admit defeat. But then he heard a noise in the distance. It was faint but familiar. It was the snatch of music played by the horn in the man's truck!

Rascal leapt to his feet. He could not see the truck and it was impossible for him to tell where the sound had come from. But then, a few seconds later, he heard the horn again. This time he was able to follow the direction of the sound.

Rascal rushed across the street and rounded a corner, just in time to see the truck turning up ahead. By the time he reached this next street, the truck was parked by the kerb. There was no sign of the man.

Rascal padded forwards carefully. The truck was parked outside a house. It was no bigger than Judy's, but the similarity ended there. Whereas Judy's house was tidy and well cared for, this one looked run-down. It was situated on a corner and Rascal couldn't see the front of it, only the side and back. There was a little garage, and between this and the house he glimpsed a patch of back yard through the wire fence.

The garden looked as poorly cared for

as the house. The ground was bare of grass and the only plants that grew were weeds. And there, lying against the wall, was a dog – a big one. It looked like a German Shepherd. But this dog was also very thin. She lay with her head forwards on the ground. There was a water bowl near her, but it was empty. There was a rope round her neck, with the other end tied to a pipe on the side of the house.

The rope hardly seemed necessary. This dog didn't look as if she had either the energy or the desire to move. Rascal knew that she must have noticed him, but she didn't lift her head or give the

slightest wag of her tail. She seemed
to have lost interest in everything. She
didn't even turn his way.

So Rascal had been right that the
man was the one who had abandoned
the puppies. And this was their mother,
Rascal was sure of it. A dog's nose
doesn't lie about such things. He gave a
little bark to attract the dog's attention,
but still she didn't look up.

Suddenly Rascal heard the sound of
voices from within the house.

'It wasn't my fault!' shouted a woman.
'How was I supposed to know it was
going to have puppies!'

'You weren't!' came the angry response, and Rascal immediately recognised this voice as belonging to the man who had shouted at him in the park. 'But that doesn't mean we had to keep 'em for weeks on end. I wanted a guard dog, not a kennels!'

The woman's voice softened. 'You got to wait a couple of weeks before you take 'em, Steve,' she said. 'Or else they won't live, that's what I heard . . . Anyway, why didn't you just take her to the animal shelter too, along with the puppies?'

The man did not say that he hadn't

even bothered to take the puppies all the way to the animal shelter, that he'd just dumped them in the park. Instead he snorted and said, 'Couldn't get much for scraggy little mongrel pups like that, could we? Couldn't give 'em away. But Lucy, she's different. She's big enough to make a good guard dog. All we gotta do is toughen her up, make her a bit meaner, and we'll be able to sell her, won't we?'

'And how are you gonna make her meaner? Lucy's a sweetie.'

'Yeah?' answered the man. 'Well, we'll see about that.'

Rascal heard footsteps approaching. He just had time to tuck himself behind the pickup truck before the door opened.

The man called Steve came out and went into the small yard. Lucy, the German Shepherd, didn't move, but her eyes followed him with wary mistrust.

The man untied the other end of the rope and gave it a hard tug. Rascal saw the rope yank on the big dog's neck and he knew how painful it must be. Slowly, the German Shepherd got to her feet.

'Come on,' snapped the man. 'I haven't got all day.'

His voice had none of the kindness or
friendliness that good dog owners use for
their pets. It was clear that in his view, if
a dog could not be of any practical use,
then it was no more than a nuisance.

He dragged the dog to the garage and
opened the doors.

'Get inside,' he said. 'Training starts
now!' And he pulled Lucy into the
garage.

The German Shepherd reacted for the first time, letting out a low, unhappy growl at the man as he dropped the rope.

'Want to bite me, do you?' snarled Steve threateningly from the doorway. 'Go ahead and try, then.'

He took a step into the garage and suddenly Rascal was filled with terrible thoughts of what this cruel man was capable of.

But what could Rascal do? Fear froze him to the spot.

Suddenly there was a noise behind him. A small car had pulled up in the middle of the road and a young sandy-haired man was leaning out of the open window.

'Hey!' he shouted to Steve. 'Are you coming or what?'

Steve hesitated for a moment, then he shut and locked the garage door before running to the waiting car. Rascal crouched even lower in his hiding spot. He didn't emerge, nor did he stop trembling, until the car was long gone.

CHAPTER 7

Slowly Rascal approached the garage door. He knew that Lucy was inside, but he couldn't hear a sound. He walked around, looking for any holes in the garage. There were none.

The only thing he could do was wait.

Surely the woman in the house would bring Lucy some food or a drink of water soon. He just would have to wait until then.

But the woman never appeared. Rascal could hear the sound of a television set from inside the house. Somehow that sound was every bit as cruel to his ears as the savage tone in Steve's voice. It meant that no one in this house really

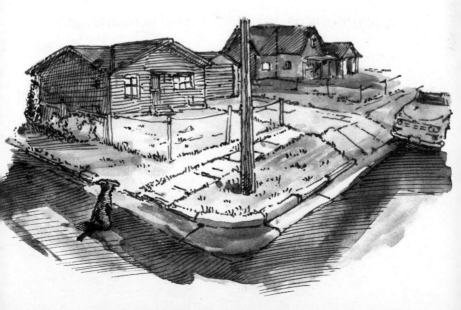

cared about the dog in their possession.

Rascal waited and waited. The shadows around him lengthened as the afternoon reached towards evening. Rascal only realised how dark it had become when a streetlight came on. Still he waited, but the man didn't return and the woman didn't emerge from the house.

And then it started to rain. At first it was just drizzle on the wind, but it soon picked up. Its drops struck at Rascal like needles. Once again he was soaked and feeling miserable. He looked around for somewhere to take shelter.

The only place was the back of the pickup truck, which was covered by a canvas roof. To get in there, he had first to jump up on to the bonnet of the car parked behind. From there he was able to jump into the higher back of the truck.

There wasn't much in there but a spare tyre, a few tools and a large, crumpled tarpaulin. This tarp wasn't as soft and warm as a blanket, but it would do. Rascal settled himself on it and just listened to the rain.

He wanted to stay alert, but there was something hypnotic about the sound of that pitter-patter on the roof, especially when he was already so weary to begin with. He didn't mean to sleep, but before too long his eyes were beginning to close and his mind was falling into unconsciousness, and there was nothing he could do about it . . .

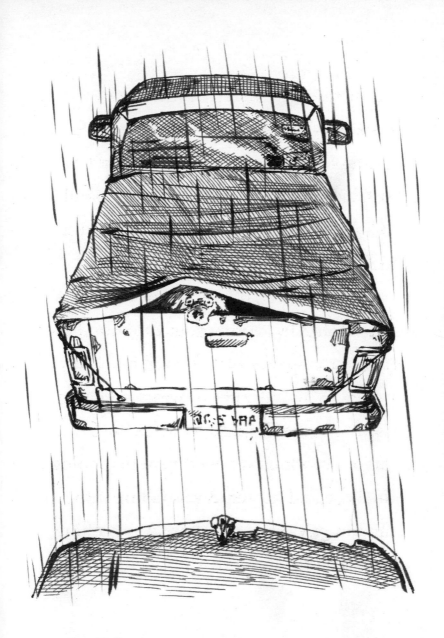

* * *

There were a few seconds of confusion in which Rascal heard voices over the drumming of the rain. Then the truck rumbled into life beneath him and he came awake properly. His first thought was to leap, but the truck was already moving too fast. It turned several corners without stopping.

On the next straight stretch, Rascal got to his feet and peeked out over the back gate of the truck. It was still raining and the darkness of evening had fully arrived. He ducked his head down quickly when he saw that there was another car following them.

The truck slowed for a moment and stopped. Rascal tensed to leap, but there wasn't time. Before he could do anything, it lurched forwards again and turned a corner. Rascal was knocked off balance, falling against the side of the truck. When he was on his feet again, the truck was going much faster. He peeked out again carefully and saw that the pickup truck was now racing along a much bigger road, a motorway of some kind.

They didn't stay on this for long,

however. The truck took the first exit and soon it was going along a dark street lined with warehouses. After one more turn, it came to a complete stop. There was the slam of a car door and the sound of another vehicle pulling up behind them.

Suddenly afraid, Rascal ducked back under the cover. Maybe if he just hid here, he could wait until the truck went back to where the German Shepherd was waiting . . .

He tried to blot out the voices from outside.

'How much stuff is there tonight?'

'Just a couple of boxes. More tomorrow, I expect.'

The first voice belonged to Steve, the second to the sandy-haired man who had driven by the house earlier in the day.

Rascal heard footsteps moving away. Maybe they were both going inside the darkened building . . . Rascal was torn between his desire to run and his desire to hide. But then there was a click as the back of the truck was unlocked and opened.

It was the other man, the sandy-haired one. He didn't look too happy

to be working in the rain like this. He pulled the canvas cover away and then his mouth opened in surprise as he saw Rascal. However, he didn't have much chance to do anything else, because the dog was ready.

Rascal rushed forwards and leapt out past the man.

'What's going on?' called Steve.

He was walking up to the truck with a large box in his hands. When he saw the dog, he set his load down quickly.

'It was in the back of the truck,' said the other man, sounding nonplussed.

But Steve was angry rather than

confused. The dog was too far away, so he bent and swept up a stone from the gutter.

'Clear off!' he yelled, and he hurled the stone at Rascal.

It missed, splashing into a puddle to one side of him.

Steve picked up an even bigger stone. 'I am getting sick to death of dogs,' he spat angrily.

Rascal didn't stick around to see if the man's aim improved. He ran into the night.

CHAPTER 8

The deepest part of Rascal's mind – the part where the wild animal lived – told him simply to flee, to get as far away from that place as he could and then keep on going. But he knew that he must not listen to that voice. He had to do something to help the three puppies. He had to do something to help their mother, Lucy.

Whatever plan he decided on, he would have to act quickly. While he had no way of guessing what Steve would do when he got home, Rascal knew he had to get the German Shepherd away from there.

That meant he had to return to the house. Perhaps the woman there would finally turn off the television and check on the dog locked in the garage . . . If Rascal was around when the garage door was opened again, there was a chance he could get the other dog out.

★ ★ ★

Rascal ran on through deserted streets
like a shadow in the rain. He knew
the direction he had to head in, back
towards the old part of town near the
river. Once he got there, it would be
easy for him to find the house again
now that he had been there before. He
turned another corner and ran past a
disused petrol station. Then he stopped.
He had reached the motorway.

Rascal knew that he had to get

across it, but he didn't know how. The
motorway was like another great river,
a river even more dangerous than the
one he had rescued the puppy from. In
both directions, two lanes of cars and
trucks raced by. It was easy to forget that
they all contained people on their way
from one place to another. To Rascal
they looked more like huge beasts
with flashing eyes and terrible roars.
Raindrops glittered like silver needles in
the headlights' glare.

The only way to cross the motorway
was to slip through the gaps between
vehicles. Rascal waited for the next car

to pass in the lane closest to him, then he stepped out.

Immediately the headlights of another car caught him. It seemed far away, but then suddenly it wasn't far away at all, it was almost upon him. The car beeped its horn and there was a screech of tyres on the wet surface.

Rascal turned and scrambled back to the side of the road. The car zipped by. He hadn't realised how fast the traffic would be travelling.

When the next gap came, Rascal stepped forwards more cautiously. This first lane was clear now, but he had to

wait until the car in the second lane of even faster traffic had gone by. It did so, but then Rascal saw that there was another car close behind it. Meanwhile, a third car was approaching in the first lane now. Panic spurted in the dog's heart. Which way should he go – forwards or backwards?

He had no more than an instant to make the decision. His legs were tensed for action, but Rascal forced himself to wait a moment longer. The car in the fast lane whizzed by and Rascal dashed forwards.

He reached the central reservation

between the two sides of the road and there he allowed himself a few moments' rest, waiting for the frantic thudding of his heart to slow down.

The traffic going in the other direction was just as heavy. Another car zoomed by and he seized his chance, dashing forwards.

It was only when he entered the second lane on this side – the last one before safety – that he realised the mistake he had made. The far lane had looked clear to him, but it wasn't. Something big was coming this way, an enormous truck of some kind. Rascal

hadn't noticed it because one of its headlights was not working and the other was higher than the headlights he'd been looking out for.

He would never make it in time. Terror held Rascal frozen in place. The truck was almost upon him and there was nothing he could do now but wait for the end . . .

At the last moment he dropped to the ground, pressing his muzzle down on the cold, wet tarmac. He did it without thinking, and then the roar of the truck filled the entire world and above him was total darkness. The rain was no longer stabbing at him. It felt as if something hot was passing overhead, something close, though it didn't quite touch him. And then in an instant the new darkness was gone and Rascal was back in the chill rain.

The truck had passed right over him! A car or even a smaller truck would surely have killed him, but this truck's undercarriage had been high enough off the ground. Each set of enormous wheels had passed on either side of him.

Rascal got unsteadily to his feet and watched the red tail lights of the truck in amazement as they sped away. His legs were still wobbly, but he ran away from the motorway as quickly as he could, before another vehicle came along.

In a short while he was back in the quiet of the smaller streets, where nothing else moved but himself and the rain.

CHAPTER 9

When he finally turned on to the
street and saw the empty parking space
outside the house, Rascal thought he
had been quick enough. He had beaten
the pickup truck back here! Perhaps
Steve would not be returning for some

time to come . . .

Then he saw that the truck *was* here
– it was just parked on the opposite side
of the road now. However, there was no
sign of the smaller car, the one the other
man had been driving.

Rascal slowed to a weary walk. Even
before he'd reached the house, the side
door opened and Steve strode out.
He had pulled on a zip-up jacket as
protection against the rain.

Steve went to the back of the pickup
truck and lowered the gate. Then he
grabbed one of the boxes that was now
in there and carried it to the garage. He

didn't put the box down but just leaned it against the door as he fiddled with the lock with his free hand. Then he pulled the door open and carried the box inside.

'You're supposed to be a guard dog,' Rascal heard him mutter. 'Aren't you supposed to bark or something?'

Rascal knew that he couldn't wait any longer. If he was going to help Lucy, it had to be now. This time he couldn't allow fear of the man to hold him back. He had to try something.

With a bark that sounded braver than he really felt, Rascal rushed forwards.

He had time to see Lucy slumped at the back of the garage before Steve turned to face the oncoming dog.

Steve's look was one of disbelief as he recognised Rascal. Then the disbelief turned to anger. But Rascal didn't come close enough for the man to lash out at him. He hung back and made as much noise as he could, barking for all he was worth. It wasn't really a plan, but part of him hoped that Lucy might be able to escape from the garage if the man continued to focus his attention on Rascal.

Steve did keep his eyes fixed on Rascal

as he bent and grabbed something from
the garage floor.

At first Rascal thought he might be
picking up something else to throw, but
he wasn't. He held a metal object, a tyre
iron. In the man's hands, the tool looked
like a dangerous weapon.

Rascal continued to snap and snarl, but he was ready to leap out of the man's range at any moment if he attacked. The dog was concentrating so hard on his confrontation with the man that he didn't even notice the sound of another car on the street behind him.

The events of the next few seconds were like a rapid series of frozen moments that hardly seemed to be connected. Rascal saw Steve running towards him, ready to strike. He felt the sting of the rain in his eyes and heard the squeal of brakes behind him as he jumped back to safety . . . Only it *wasn't*

to safety, because suddenly there was
a dreadful thud, the worst pain in the
entire world engulfed him and he was
tumbling through the air. He landed in a
crumpled heap at the kerb.

The car had hit him.

Rascal just lay there. He had never felt agony like this before. The pain in his back legs had become the centre of the world for him.

'I didn't see it,' the sandy-haired man was saying in a high, panicky voice. He was standing at the door of his car. 'It just ran out into the road!'

But this wasn't the person Rascal was concerned about. A few moments later, Steve appeared. Behind him, a window in the house opened and a thin woman appeared.

'What's going on?' she shouted, but Steve ignored her.

'You must have a death wish or somethin', dog,' he snarled at Rascal.

There was nothing the dog could do. He couldn't get away. He couldn't even move his back legs without searing pain.

The man loomed over him now, a cold anger burning in his eyes.

But then suddenly there was another noise from behind the man. It was Lucy, the German Shepherd. No longer gentle, she didn't make a sound except for a low growl in her throat. Her teeth were bared. Despite her thinness, she was a fearsome sight.

Steve turned. His eyes widened with fear, but he stood his ground. His arm went back, ready to strike, but he was too slow. The next instant, the German Shepherd launched herself through the air. Her jaws clamped on to his forearm.

Steve let out a startled cry and dropped his makeshift weapon.

'Help me!' he shouted, but his 'friend' was already running back towards his car.

The German Shepherd wouldn't let go, however much Steve tried to shake her off. But then, in desperation, he whirled around and the dog did finally loosen her grip. As the other car zoomed off, Steve began to run towards the house. But the German Shepherd didn't let him get far before she jumped up and brought him tumbling to the ground.

The man didn't try to get up again. He lay on his side and put his arms over his face, bringing his knees up to his stomach. Lucy was barking at him. The noise was terrible, but she wasn't biting him – just making a lot of noise to keep him curled up in this position.

She didn't have to do this for long, because soon Rascal heard the wail of sirens in the distance. They grew louder and louder. Perhaps someone had heard the sound of the car accident and called the police . . .

Rascal tried to hold on to consciousness, but the pain was spreading out from his back legs and, as it did so, it blotted out all other thoughts. Finally, there was nothing he could do but let himself fall back into the terrible black hole of the pain.

CHAPTER 10

Before he opened his eyes, Rascal heard
voices. They seemed to fade in and out,
but the pain was always there. He felt
it in his whole body, felt it with each
breath he took, but the pain was worst
in one of his back legs.

'She's far too thin,' said a man's voice
with barely controlled anger. 'I can feel
her spine. This dog has been underfed
for weeks. If it's true that she had a litter
recently, that makes things even worse.
A dog that is suckling puppies should be
given more food than usual.'

Rascal's eyes fluttered open. He was
lying on a table in a brightly lit, low-

ceilinged room. There were medical instruments all around and framed pictures of happy pets and their smiling families on the walls.

If he arched his neck a little, he could see where the two voices were coming from – an adjoining room that contained a man and a woman in blue medical uniforms. They were both examining Lucy.

'This sort of thing is unforgivable,' continued the man. 'The courts should throw the book at people who neglect and abuse dogs like this.'

The woman gave a grim smile of

agreement. 'I know what you mean,' she said. 'But the man who did this won't get away with it. Apparently, when the police arrived, they found stolen goods in his truck and garage – laptops and smartphones, stuff like that.'

'But what about the puppies?' asked the man. As he spoke, he placed a small bowl of food in front of Lucy, who began to eat it eagerly.

'The shelter placed them with a volunteer foster parent,' said the woman. 'Apparently, they haven't even been fully weaned yet and they aren't taking to the formula very well. We'll see them

soon enough. When she heard that
we've got the mother here at the clinic,
the volunteer said she'd bring them in
herself.'

They both smiled down at the dog.
Lucy had finished the bowl of food and
was clearly ready for more.

'In a little while,' said the vet kindly. 'You've got to take it slowly when your stomach has shrunk like this.'

The woman in the blue uniform turned and came into the room where Rascal was.

'How's this one doing?' she asked.

'Not so good,' answered another woman behind him.

Until this, Rascal hadn't realised that there was anyone in the room with him.

'There weren't any tags found on the street, then?' asked the first woman.

'Uh-uh,' came the answer. 'He must be a stray.' The woman sighed. 'His back leg is broken for certain, a compound fracture. We'd need to do an X-ray to check his spine and ribs. But if there's no owner, I'm afraid we'll have to put him down. It's the kindest thing.' Her voice was sad.

'You'll do no such thing,' cut in another voice, this one familiar. It was Judy! She stood at the door, still wearing a long raincoat and holding an umbrella in one hand. 'Just do what you can for him. I'll take care of the bill and I'll look after him afterwards.'

It was painful for him to do it, but Rascal arched his neck even more. He had to, and it was worth it, despite the stab of pain that ran through him. It was worth it because he caught a glimpse of the three puppies reunited with Lucy.

The German Shepherd was licking them and they were trying to clamber on to her.

It was enough for Rascal. He knew that they would all be OK now.

Then he felt a firm hand on his forehead. He opened his eyes to see a woman in a surgical mask looking down at him.

'OK, we'll do our best, but I can't give any guarantees,' she said grimly. 'This poor guy isn't in very good shape.' Next she spoke directly to Rascal. 'It's going to be all right, boy,' she said. 'This is just going to relax you and let you sleep while we make you all better.'

Rascal felt a new kind of pain as a needle was inserted into his haunches, but then the other, bigger pain began to fade and melt away.

The last thing he saw was the look of concern on Judy's face above him. And then that too faded. It was almost as if the world around him was slipping away, as darkness folded itself around him and pulled him down to a place where there was no more pain at all.

CHAPTER 11

Rascal's owner, Joel, woke with a start.

He blinked his eyes in confusion. He couldn't remember his dream, but his heart was thudding wildly and he was left with a terrible sense that something was wrong. The feeling didn't disappear even when he told himself not to be so silly, that it was just a nightmare.

Something *was* wrong and it had to do with Rascal.

Joel looked at his alarm clock – it was just after two o'clock in the morning. Everyone else in the house would be asleep,

but Joel knew that he would never be able to get back to sleep now.

He climbed out of bed and went to the window. No stars were visible through the blanket of clouds in the sky. Somehow, alone in the quiet and darkness, Joel felt his optimism of the previous day vanish. That had been a daydream, a thing of the sun. Here, now, in the middle of the starless night, the terrible truth seemed to press down on him.

Rascal was gone, gone forever.

Will Rascal ever get home to Joel?
Find out in his final adventure,

RACING AGAINST TIME.

Turn the page for an extract . . .

CHAPTER 1

Winter had arrived and the days were
at their shortest. By the time Rascal
saw lights up ahead, it had been dark
for a few hours. A small flame of hope
sparked inside the dog at the sight of
them – perhaps he'd find a place to rest

and shelter from the cold there? But
it was hard to keep that hope alive. As
night had fallen, so had the temperature.
The chill wind buffeted him, and the
occasional flake of snow in the air
hinted at even worse weather on the
way. Pushing through his tiredness,
Rascal continued towards the glow of
the electric lights.

It wasn't easy to be cold and alone like this again. The dog had been forced to delay his long journey several weeks earlier, when his back leg had been fractured by a car. Luckily for Rascal, Judy, a volunteer for the local animal shelter and a true dog lover, had taken him in. He had grown accustomed to being warm and well-fed at her house while his leg mended.

And yet, Rascal hadn't been able to shake the restless feeling at the back of his mind. Judy was a great owner, but she wasn't *his* owner. She was kind and loving to him, but she was that way with all dogs. That's why Judy volunteered to act as a foster owner for any dogs from the shelter that needed special attention. Every time Rascal found himself relaxing and starting to enjoy life with Judy, an image of his old master, Joel – his true master – would pop into his mind, No, he knew he had to continue on his journey home, just as soon as he could.

At last, the day came when Rascal was taken to the vet's and the splint on his leg removed. He touched the floor gingerly with his back paw. It felt good to walk on all fours once again, even if the muscles of the injured leg felt weak through lack of use.

It was time to move on.

Judy was sitting in her favourite chair with the newspaper when Rascal came up to her and pawed her knee.

'You're not looking for more food, are you?' she asked. 'I've never seen a dog eat as much as you did this morning!'

Rascal just looked at this woman who had shown him such kindness. In a rush he leaned forwards and gave her face a lick.

'Get off, you great soppy thing!' laughed Judy.

Rascal wandered out to the garden – out of Judy's line of vision. He looked at the fence ahead of him. He had jumped over this fence once before, but that had been before his back leg had been injured. It might not be so easy now.

Rascal took a breath and charged towards the fence. As before, he sailed over. The instant he landed on the pavement on the other side, he knew that his status had changed. He was not a pet any more. He was a stray dog again, trying to find his way home.

The rest of the day was a blur of sore feet and aching bones and a growing emptiness in his stomach, as Rascal headed west. It didn't take long to leave the town behind him, and then he was crossing open land. A large highway ran straight west, and he kept it in sight as if navigating along the banks of a mighty river.

Knowing that he must find shelter before he could give in to sleep, Rascal carried on long after the sky had darkened. And that's when he saw the lights up ahead . . .

CHAPTER 2

They belonged to a small café, set back from the highway, and a small motel just beyond that.

Rascal could smell the food from a long way away. Although he had eaten as much as he possibly could at Judy's house that morning, he was back to his usual condition – starving. Perhaps he could find something to eat in the rubbish bins round the back of the café?

But, as he neared the building, the front door opened and someone stepped out. He was young and his long hair was pulled back in a loose ponytail. The light jacket he wore wasn't enough to keep out the cold evening air.

The man had a kind, open face and Rascal thought that it was worth a try to see if he had any food. The dog gave a friendly bark.

'Hey, boy,' said the man, rubbing his

hands together to warm them.

Rascal barked again, wagging his tail. Then he sat down expectantly.

The man hesitated, then grinned. 'I get it,' he said. 'It's food you're after, right?'

He opened the plastic container he had been carrying under one arm, and smiled.

'You do realise these leftovers were going to be my lunch for tomorrow?'

He pulled a few strips of bacon out and tossed them to Rascal, who scoffed them down in an instant. They were cold, overdone almost to a crisp, and completely and utterly delicious.

'I guess that's why they call them doggy bags,' laughed the man. He began to walk across the parking lot to the motel that adjoined the café. 'You'd better go home now, doggy,' he said over his shoulder. 'Radio said worse weather's on the way ...'

Rascal watched as the man entered

one of the rooms on the ground level of the motel. Then the dog took up position outside the café entrance. Maybe he would be just as lucky with the next person who came out? He waited and waited, but no one came.

At last, a face did appear at the café door. It was a woman, but she didn't come out; she just locked the door from the inside, gave Rascal a suspicious look, and then turned round, clicking off the light at the front of the café. There would be no more food tonight.

Rascal turned his attention to finding a place to sleep. The doorway of the café

offered little protection against the
wind. Rascal padded round to the
side of the building. There was a large
rubbish skip here. It wasn't much, but
the narrow gap between it and the wall
offered a little shelter. Wearily, Rascal
crawled in.

It was so cold now that Rascal
could hardly get to sleep.
When he finally did drop
off, his dreams were shot
through with frost
and snow.

Books should be returned or renewed by the last date above. Renew by phone **08458 247 200** or online *www.kent.gov.uk/libs*

Libraries & Archives